PINOCULA

THE CREATURE
FROM MY
CLOSET

OBERT SKYE

SQUARE
FISH

Christy Ottaviano Books

Henry Holt and Company • New York

SQUARE
FISH

An imprint of Macmillan Publishing Group, LLC
175 Fifth Avenue
New York, NY 10010
mackids.com

Our books may be purchased in bulk for promotional, educational, or business
use. Please contact your local bookseller or the Macmillan Corporate and
Premium Sales Department at (800) 221-7945 ext. 5442 or by
e-mail at MacmillanSpecialMarkets@macmillan.com.

Library of Congress Cataloging-in-Publication Data
Skye, Obert, author, illustrator.
Pinocula / Obert Skye. —
p.   cm. — (The creature from my closet ; book 3)
Summary: Things are going pretty well for Rob Burnside until Pinocula—a
cross between Pinocchio and a vampire—emerges from
his closet, lying, joking, and doing his best to drive Rob crazy.
ISBN 978-1-250-11501-0 (paperback)   ISBN 978-1-46684-565-7 (ebook)
[1. Monsters—Fiction.   2. Conduct of life—Fiction.   3. Books and
reading—Fiction.   4. Schools—Fiction.   5. Family life—Fiction.
6. Humorous stories.]   I. Title.
PZ7.S62877Pin 2013   [Fic]—dc23   2013017882

Originally published in the United States by Christy Ottaviano
Books/Henry Holt and Company
First Square Fish Edition: 2017
Book designed by Véronique Lefèvre Sweet
Square Fish logo designed by Filomena Tuosto

1   3   5   7   9   10   8   6   4   2

AR: 4.6 / LEXILE: 780L

For my remarkable Naomi—
Thanks for making everything
in life more fun

CONTENTS

PINOCULA
THE CREATURE
FROM MY
CLOSET

CHAPTER 1

LET ME FILL YOU IN

Okay, here's the deal—

I'M PRETTY SORRY ABOUT WHAT I DID.

Beginning with an apology is probably not the best way to start this book, but I think it's the smart thing to do. That way when you get to the part where I messed up, I can just remind you I already said I'm sorry and you might give me a break.

Before I tell you what I'm sorry about, it might be wise to fill you in on a few other things. If you're new to my journals and drawings, you probably don't know my name. Well, it's . . .

ROBERT COLUMBO BURNSIDE!

My mom is the only one who calls me by my full name, and that's only when she's really ticked off. The rest of the time she calls me Ribert. Most people call me Rob. I'm a student at Softrock

Middle School in a town called Temon. Our school's a little behind the times. According to my principal we just barely got our own Facebook page.

Principal Smelt's a pretty good principal. He plays the pan flute and is in a two-man band named Leftover Angst. Still, I'm not adding my school as a friend on Facebook. I just don't want anyone to see how boring my page is or that my only friend at the moment is my father.

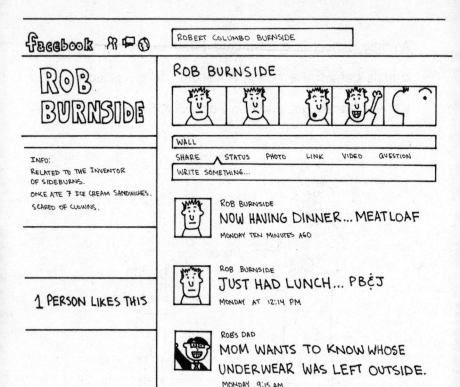

ROBERT COLUMBO BURNSIDE

ROB BURNSIDE

ROB BURNSIDE

INFO:
RELATED TO THE INVENTOR
OF SIDEBURNS.
ONCE ATE 7 ICE CREAM SANDWICHES.
SCARED OF CLOWNS.

1 PERSON LIKES THIS

WALL

SHARE   STATUS   PHOTO   LINK   VIDEO   QUESTION

WRITE SOMETHING...

ROB BURNSIDE
NOW HAVING DINNER... MEATLOAF
MONDAY TEN MINUTES AGO

ROB BURNSIDE
JUST HAD LUNCH... PB&J
MONDAY AT 12:14 PM

ROB'S DAD
MOM WANTS TO KNOW WHOSE UNDERWEAR WAS LEFT OUTSIDE.
MONDAY 9:15 AM

I have a pretty normal family. Of course you couldn't tell that from our last family photo. The photographer arranged us in an awkward way, and my little brother, Tuffin, kept lifting his shirt. So now it looks like Libby is showing the world her stomach.

4

It's my favorite family picture ever. My older sister hates it, but Libby hates a lot of things. The only thing she truly likes is herself. And if you ask her what she's into she always answers...

I'M REALLY INTO MYSELF.

Tuffin's not really into himself, he's more into mischief. Lately he's been slipping strange things into the sandwiches I bring to school for lunch.

My mom tells me to be thankful for the cute things that Tuffin does.

I like Tuffin, but it's hard to feel thankful after biting into a peanut butter and rubber band sandwich. I guess my mom has to say things like that though. She's a mom—a mom who spends a lot of her time taking naps on the couch. She's almost always wearing her robe, and she claims that having children makes her tired. That's probably true, but how much effort does it take to give me orders while I'm trying to sneak away to hang out with my friends?

DO THE DISHES!

My dad doesn't ever nap—he's too busy doing a million things to have the time to lie down. He's

always excited about life. He has glasses, and he
wears a suit and tie because, as he puts it,

My dad owns a small company that sells playground
equipment to schools. His first name is Earl, and he
loves his job.

Sometimes he uses me and my friends to test things. Three days ago he had us try out a big swing called an Exer-Glide. It was an unusual swing that looks like a metal cage. It's supposed to hold one person, and you pump with your arms, not your legs.

My dad claimed it was an extra-safe swing because kids couldn't jump out and hurt themselves. Well, maybe it was hard to jump out, but it didn't seem very safe. My friends and I had a difficult time getting it to move.

My dad had a really tough time pulling all of us out. If you ask me, though, I think it was just as tough having to listen to his lecture about us...

I should at least mention Janae. It might be important for you to know who she is. Janae lives next door, and I like her way more than she likes me. I can barely walk right when she's around. Yesterday I saw her in the hall at school and tried to wave. While waving, I tripped over a small kid getting stuff from his bottom locker and fell flat on my nose.

I actually tried to stay home from school this morning because my nose was so swollen, but my mom didn't let me. So I guess she's partly to blame. If I hadn't gone to school today, I wouldn't have made the mistake I've already apologized for. Sadly, going back in time is not yet an option.

CHAPTER 2

THE STARTING LIE

Since my time machine didn't work, I was forced to go to school today, and here's what happened. After lunch we had a school assembly. The speaker was a Temon city worker with poofy hair. He came to talk to us about his job working at the city parks. He talked a lot about watering things. He went on and on about how challenging his work was and then he said...

EVERY DAY, I COME HOME POOPED FROM DOING MY DUTY.

I didn't want to laugh, but I couldn't help it—words like *duty* and *pooped* are immaturity power words. The second I laughed, the whole crowd began to laugh with me. It took Principal Smelt ten minutes to get everyone calmed down, and Mr. Poofy Hair stormed off the stage in a huff. I shouldn't have laughed, but city workers need to be careful about what they say in front of middle schoolers.

I was raised not to joke about gross things. When I was really little, my mom made me watch *The Adventures of Bathroom Billy*. It's an educational show about a talking toilet named Billy that helps kids know how to properly act in the bathroom.

DON'T SAY POO—SAY NUMBER 2. THAT'S WHAT ALL POLITE KIDS DO.

I had failed Bathroom Billy, and my laughing had ruined the whole assembly. The speaker was mad, the teachers were mad, and lots of the students were mad because we had to go back to our classes. Principal Smelt was so upset his ears were steaming. As I was walking out of the assembly, he stopped me in the hall to ask me if I had anything to do with what he was calling...

THE GREAT ASSEMBLY DISASTER!

Principal Smelt was angrier than I had ever seen him before. His face was red, and his mustache looked sweaty. He wanted me to name names. He wanted me to tell him everyone I had seen laughing.

He also informed me that the city worker with the poofy hair was actually his second cousin.

THIS IS PERSONAL!

I felt bad, but I also felt like I should keep my mouth shut. I didn't see how it would help for me to speak up and let him know it was my fault. Principal Smelt wiped his forehead and asked,

DO YOU HAVE ANY IDEA WHO STARTED THE LAUGHING?

Okay, this is the spot where I need to remind you that I've already apologized. I shouldn't have laughed at what my principal's second cousin had said, but I especially shouldn't have opened my mouth and lied about it.

IT DEFINITELY WASN'T ME.

Principal Smelt stared at my swelling nose for a moment. He sighed louder than anyone I had ever heard sigh before and then smiled weakly. He patted me on the shoulder and called me a good egg.

I'M GOOD.

Principal Smelt concluded our conversation by informing me that he needed to find and punish the students who laughed first. He assigned me to do some "sleuthing" and discover who the "instigator" was. I said okay, even though I didn't completely understand what he was asking.

So, after dinner tonight, I looked up the word *instigator* in my mom's old dictionary. According to the definition, I was one. I had instigated the laughing, and I followed that laughing by lying. Principal Smelt was wrong—I was a *bad* egg.

I'M OOZING.

I sat down on my bed and stared at my closet door. Beardy, the little face on my brass closet doorknob, looked like he was disappointed in me.

Beardy made me think of Wonkenstein and Hairy. I missed the first two creatures that had come out of my closet. It'd be great to have them here now so that I could explain myself to somebody.

Wonk and Hairy had made my life pretty crazy, but they had been fun to have around. Not a day went by when I didn't wish they'd at least return for a visit. I've tried to get back into my closet to see if anyone else might be in there, but Beardy keeps it locked tight.

I wanted to lie down on my bed and rest, but the word *lie* made me uncomfortable. I opened my bedroom window to climb out and go see my friends. As I was climbing out, I heard a scratching noise coming from behind my closet door. I spun around. My closet gurgled and burped loudly. Light began to seep out from beneath the door. To make things more unsettling, Beardy was shining.

I reached out to turn Beardy. He was locked and hot, causing me to yelp. I stepped back and stared at my closet door. My insides tumbled and turned like grapes in a washing machine.

21

My closet made a large noise as something shifted and moved behind the door. My poor stomach felt beat up.

I stared at my closet and waited for the door to pop open. I tested Beardy, but he was being stubborn and refused to budge.

The glowing stopped, and eventually my closet
door looked normal again. It was only seven o'clock,
but I was tired. I had gone to bed late last night
because my nose still hurt and I couldn't get
comfortable in my bed. So I had stayed up and
watched a movie. The one I saw was about a spy
who had the ability to pop his eyes out and use them
to spy on people from far away. It was called...

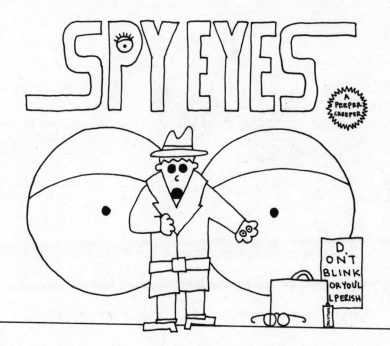

The eyes were able to bounce and do all kinds of freaky things like see through walls and make little bruises on people by pelting them. In one of the scenes, there was a guy combing his hair in a bathroom and one of the eyes was spying on him from inside his tube of toothpaste. When he went to brush his teeth, the eye squeezed out and attacked the man.

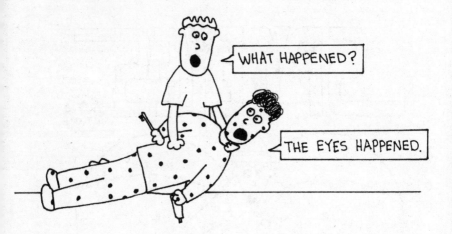

It was a pretty stupid movie, but after watching I was scared to brush my teeth and go to bed. I was worried that some eyes might bounce up on me.

Tonight, however, I was so tired I didn't care if someone's entire face was after me. I told my family to leave me alone, changed into one of my dad's old concert T-shirts, and climbed into bed. I pulled out the Thumb Buddies comic book I kept hidden under my mattress and read two quick pages.

I wanted to find out what happened to Baby Stabs, but I fell asleep. I woke up five hours later at midnight. My room was pitch black, and the house was quiet. I could hear my fat dog, Puck, snoring softly down the hall. My bladder was whining about being full.

I'M GOING TO BURST!

I was not going to get up and go to the bathroom. Not with stray eyeballs bouncing around. I closed my eyes, and as I was trying to drift back to sleep, I heard a soft...

SQWEET.

My eyelids snapped open. I turned my head from side to side, wondering if there was a stray eyeball bouncing toward me.

SQWEET!

The noise sounded like something wooden climbing up onto my bed. My heart went into overdrive as the noise got louder.

SQWEET!

I felt something cold brush over my face. Quickly I reached to the side of my bed and grabbed my baseball bat. There was a loud crunching noise as I stood up and flipped on my desk light. I had grabbed the bat to swing at the intruder, but that was no longer necessary. The intruder had beat me to it.

Hanging from the end of my wooden bat was a brand-new visitor. I couldn't decide if I should scream or smile. My closet had done it again. I noticed the closet door was now open about an inch and Beardy looked smug.

Holding the bat, with the creature still dangling, I moved over and softly closed my bedroom door. The last thing I wanted to do was wake my parents. I was nervous, but I was also happy to see that my closet had produced something new.

The little guy's teeth were stuck in the wood, and he was having a difficult time getting them loose. I swung the bat gently, and he broke free. He fell off the bat, and I slipped backward onto my purple beanbag. The creature smiled at me. I should let you know that it was a far more mischievous smile than Wonk or Hairy had ever smiled. I looked at the creature to determine what books had helped shape him. He had a partial cape and jet-black hair. One arm and leg looked like they were made from wood, and his nose was pointy and long. He had on a small, tapered hat, and there were strings hanging from his left arm. He looked like a vampire that was closely related to the Pinocchio family.

I set him on my desk so that I could study him better.

I think I was about to say something important when a black object flew out of my closet and brushed the back of my head. My heart went nuts.

I turned around and frantically searched the room for what had assaulted me. A small shadow darted across my view and into the corner behind my beanbag.

Pinocula wasn't spilling the beans. Whatever it was darted back up, flew over my head, and smacked against the window. I grabbed my pillow and slipped off the case. Holding it like a net, I dove toward the flying intruder.

KAMIKAZE!

The fluttering dark spot zigged and I missed. I slid up against my closet door with a thud as whatever it was flapped madly above me. I tried to grab it, but all I saw was a cloud of wings and my hands. As I was swatting it away, it bit me on the right thumb.

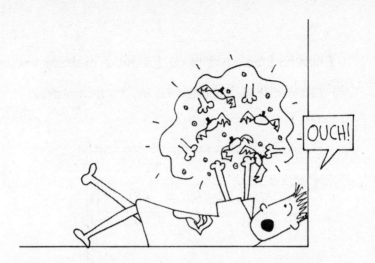

Pinocula whistled softly, and the flying object darted away from me. It hovered in the air a few feet to the side of Pinocula and flapped its wings. I stood up and with one swoop bagged the flying menace in my pillowcase. It thrashed and jiggled. The sack kept smacking up against me as I tried to hold it closed.

33

I had no idea what to do. To make matters worse, my dad suddenly knocked on my bedroom door.

I was far from all right, and unless I moved quickly, I was about to be in big trouble.

CHAPTER 3

BLACKOUTS AND GLOW BANDS

I turned around, and Pinocula had his hands out.
Without thinking, I gave him the pillowcase and
grabbed my blanket to hide them both. Pinocula
pulled the bat-bird thing out of the bag and shoved
it under his hat.

My bedroom door began to open. I tried to pull my blanket over Pinocula, but I was too slow—my dad was coming in! I wrapped my arm around Pinocula, holding the blanket with my other hand while sucking on my thumb to hide the bite mark.

I think my dad was pretty upset about being woken up in the middle of the night, but he seemed more concerned about me sucking my thumb and holding a blankie and a doll.

I was worried that Pinocula would move and give me away, but he just hung limp in my arms like a half-wooden doll.

My dad changed his line of questioning. He now wanted to know why I was awake and making noise after midnight. When I wasn't able to explain myself properly, he asked . . .

I needed to act carefully—there weren't too many times in my life when I had seen my dad mad. For the most part he was smiley and too busy pointing out positive stuff to be negative. But the one thing that makes him cranky is when he doesn't get enough sleep. Those are dangerous times because he doesn't know how to ground people right. My mom was good at it.

My dad, on the other hand, had so little experience with grounding that when he did try, the punishments were always way out of whack. Last summer he grounded Libby from TV for two years, just because she forgot to take the trash out. I knew that if I wasn't careful, my dad might ground me from eating for the next six months. So, I figured if a lie had helped get me out of trouble with Principal Smelt, a lie might help me here. I stood up and set Pinocula under my blanket. I looked at the baseball bat and came up with an okay lie.

I WAS PRACTICING MY BASEBALL SWING. I'M SCARED THAT I'M NOT GOING TO MAKE THE TEAM.

WHAT? YOU'RE TRYING OUT FOR A TEAM?

I knew it'd work. My dad had a weak spot for team sports. He put his arm around me and told me how proud he was. He congratulated me for being a go-getter. He then told me that anything was possible and promised he'd show me some pictures tomorrow of when he was a kid and he was on a baseball team.

My dad left, closing my door softly behind him and quietly whistling "Take Me Out to the Ball Game." Pinocula jumped down from my bed and looked at me.

It wasn't. I had never really been into vampires. I knew my older sister, Libby, and all the girls at my school were crazy about them, but they liked the kind that sparkled and were moody. I had seen some movies, but I had never read a Dracula book. I knew even less about Pinocchio. What I did know was that my closet had cooked up something cool.

I set Pinocula on my desk. His long nose twitched and wiggled. He smiled at me, and his two sharp fangs glistened under the light of my lamp.

I told Pinocula all about myself. Most of it was the truth. I might have exaggerated about how good a basketball player I was, but the rest of it was pretty accurate. I told him that I missed Wonk and Hairy and that I was glad he was here. I pointed out how he sort of reminded me of LEGOs.

And how I always used to get specific sets, but in the end they just became one big, mixed-up pile.

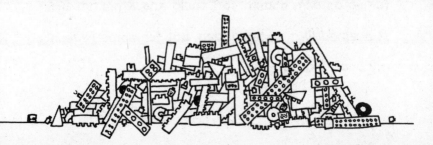

Pinocula looked at me as if he were confused.

As I was telling him more about myself, Pinocula's hat wiggled and he reached up to straighten it. I had forgotten about the small thing that had bit me. I asked to see what was under his cap, but Pinocula insisted there was nothing. I thought about faking an arm spasm so I could knock his hat off. It seemed like a stupid idea, but for some reason my brain liked it.

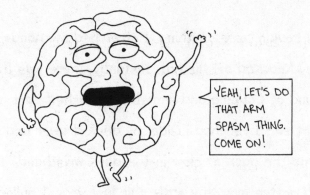

I shook my shoulders and flung my right arm toward Pinocula's hat. Pinocula ducked, and my hand hit my desk lamp. The lamp crashed to the floor, and the room went dark. Pinocula liked the change.

I couldn't *see* anything. I stretched my hands, and they knocked off his hat. Instantly, there was the sound of flapping and something brushed past my right ear. I reached inside my desk drawer and found the pack of glow-in-the-dark wristbands I had gotten from the state fair last year. I pulled a couple of them out and cracked the tubes so they lit up. Pinocula really liked them.

Pinocula laughed. I didn't think it was particularly funny, but I smiled to make him feel okay about his sense of humor. I stood up from my chair and began to slowly search my room for whatever had popped out of his hat. There was no sign of anything, and the window was still open from before.

I THINK IT GOT AWAY.

YOU THINK WHAT GOT AWAY?

WHATEVER WAS UNDER YOUR HAT.

THERE WASN'T ANYTHING UNDER MY HAT.

Pinocula had a really hard time telling the truth. He jumped off my desk and looked around the room. His left foot clicked while his right leg and left arm rattled like hollow wooden pipes. He stopped in front of the closet and held up his glowing wrist. Beardy shielded his eyes.

I tried to explain to Pinocula that I was beginning to feel a little sick and should probably rest up for school in the morning, but that just made him more excited.

YOU GO TO SCHOOL LIKE A REAL BOY?

I THINK SO.

Pinocula wanted to go with me to school. I thought it sounded like a bad idea, but I told him if he let me get some sleep, I'd think about it. I was worried he might mess something up while I was sleeping, but he said...

I WON'T DO ANYTHING. CROSS MY HEART.

Pinocula took a seat on my beanbag, and I crawled back into bed. I fell asleep wondering if

he had a heart and just what other bits and pieces
he might *be* made of.

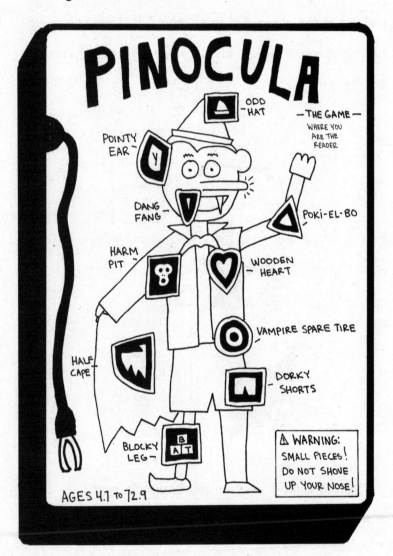

CHAPTER 4

STRANGE RELATIONS

I woke up to the sound of my little brother singing right next to my bed. Lately Tuffin had been making up songs and singing them loudly.

NO-SHIRT SONG! NO-SHIRT SONG! WEARING PANTS WITH NO SHIRT ON!

His songs didn't make much sense. I told him to kindly shut his mouth while I tried to open my eyelids. My eyes hurt and my bones were aching, but I got out of bed and ready for school. Looking out my window, I saw that the sky was filled with dark clouds. While brushing my teeth, I noticed the Band-Aid on my thumb. My mind quickly began to clear out the cobwebs of forgetfulness from sleep.

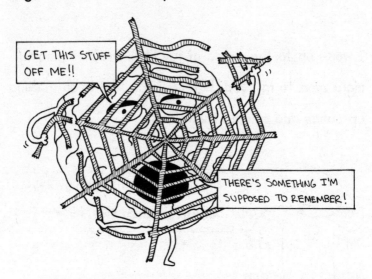

Pinocula! I ran back into my room and searched everywhere for him. I checked my brother's room

and my parents'. No luck. I checked Libby's. She
was no help.

I couldn't find Pinocula anywhere. The only thing
I could think of was that he escaped through my
window. I stared out the glass. There was nothing
outside my window besides the empty rock island in
the middle of the cul-de-sac and the abandoned
Awful House where the Pangs used to live.

Looking at the Pangs' old house made me shiver.
After Wonkenstein had caused Mr. Pang's toes to grow
long, Mr. Pang thought his house was haunted. So he
and his son, Ogre, had moved. It was spooky but cool
to have an empty house in the neighborhood now.

I left my room and went looking for my mom. I
needed to act sick so I could get out of going to
school and keep searching for Pinocula.

3 (May) 7

I tried a few more excuses, but Mom wasn't budging. So I gave up and left my house. On the bus I sat next to my best friend, Trevor. His glasses were crooked as usual, and he seemed excited. He was carrying a model of a wolf he had made for one of his classes. He was pretty geeked up about the project. He started to tell me all kinds of facts about wolves, but I interrupted him.

I asked Trevor if he was aware that not many closets in the world had old laboratory supplies and books in them that dripped and smooshed together to produce small, living, mixed-up creatures. He wasn't listening.

Trevor's thoughts were too wrapped up in wolves to get his attention. My friends Aaron, Jack, Rourk, and Teddy were sitting behind us. I considered telling them, but they were busy with their own conversation.

My first class of the day was reading. My teacher,
Ms. Bela, is way strict and always talks about books
as if they'll save the world. She thinks there's nothing
more important than reading.

We were halfway through class when the door
opened and Principal Smelt walked in with a surprise.

I...I... couldn't believe it! Pinocula was wearing some of Tuffin's clothes, and he had on my mom's sunglasses.

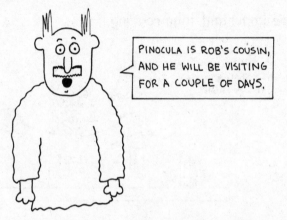

PINOCULA IS ROB'S COUSIN, AND HE WILL BE VISITING FOR A COUPLE OF DAYS.

Everyone turned and looked at me. I didn't know what to say, so I just sat there looking like a piece of dead wood.

I'M STUMPED.

Principal Smelt told the class that according to the official-looking letter Pinocula had given him, Pinocula had an unusual condition that required him to wear sunglasses and not be in the light.

All the girls ohhhhhed, as if that were adorable. Pinocula walked down the aisle and climbed into the desk next to me.

Ms. Bela welcomed Pinocula and then went back to talking about how reading was the only real subject that mattered. As soon as everyone was looking away, I leaned over and whispered,

I tried to explain to Pinocula what a horrible idea this was, but he wouldn't hear it. To make matters worse, he kept answering questions that he clearly didn't know the answer to.

As soon as class was over, I picked up Pinocula and ran down the hall to the empty gym. I put him on one of the bleachers and began to pepper him with questions.

Pinocula explained that while I was sleeping he
had explored my house and found his new clothes.
After that he slipped out my window and went
around the neighborhood searching for a decent
coffin to rest in.

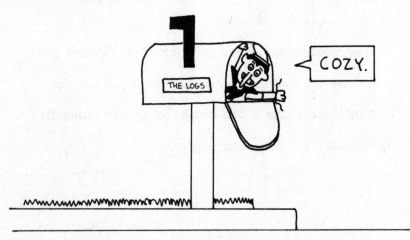

When the sun came up, Pinocula began to feel
guilty about not going to school. Apparently, the
Pinocchio part of him longed to learn. The vampire
part of him wasn't all that keen on schooling, but he
thought there might be a lot of tasty wooden rulers
and pencils for him to bite.

While we were arguing, two girls came into the gym to hang up a poster for the dance that was coming up this Friday. Our first middle school dance. It was only three days away, and most of the girls were jazzed about it while most of the boys were scared. The two girls looked at us as they hung up the poster. They were kind of upset about the "Under the Sea" theme Principal Smelt had picked.

Pinocula started to point out problems with

Twilight.

The two girls looked hurt by what he was saying, so I put my hand over his mouth and pulled him away to my next class.

It was weird, but for some reason all the students and staff of Softrock Middle School just accepted Pinocula as my cousin. At lunch, even Trevor fell for it.

YOU DIDN'T TELL ME YOUR COUSIN WAS COMING.

After lunch, Pinocula and I went to the school library to see if I could find some books about him. They didn't have *Pinocchio*, and thanks to *Twilight* and everyone's obsession with vampires, all the vampire books were checked out. Every girl I knew loved the un-dead, including the librarian.

I had to stop Pinocula from taking a bite of the wooden counter, and we left empty-handed.

During shop class, I worked on the spice rack I was making while Pinocula made a mirror. It was sort of a silly thing for him to make, given the vampire part of him couldn't be seen in his reflection.

While I was getting my stuff at the end of the day, Pinocula wanted to test out my locker as a coffin. I set him in to see how it felt.

Janae was coming, so I quickly slammed the door. I was worried about how out of place he'd look resting in my coffin-locker. Janae saw me slam the locker and asked if I was mad about something. I should have just said no, but instead I lied.

Janae stood there staring at me. She looked like
she was waiting for me to say something else
dumb . . . so I did. To make it worse, I pointed at
her while I said it.

Janae looked like someone had just told her that her cat died. I hadn't meant to say it that way. I wanted Janae to go *to the dance* with me, not *go with me*. I tried to explain my way out of it.

I DON'T MEAN GO WITH ME. I MEAN GO TO THE DANCE WITH ME — LIKE FRIENDS. SINCE WE'RE NEIGHBORS AND IT'LL SAVE ON GAS. THERE WILL BE MUSIC AND DANCING. I'M A SUPER-GOOD DANCER. IN FACT, I TOOK DANCE CLASSES FOR FIVE YEARS. I EVEN WON AN AWARD.

My mouth wouldn't shut up. I begged my brain to stop the madness, but it was no use. I continued talking and talking, and Janae kept looking more and more worried. I was telling her dumber things than the things I usually said. I knew I needed to say something good or Janae might never speak to me again. So I threw out a new lie.

Janae smiled wide. She asked me if it'd be okay for two of her friends to ride with us in the limo. I had to use both of my hands and some of my toes to answer her.

Janae thanked me and smiled again. She walked off, leaving me alone. It had all happened so fast I barely had time to realize what a huge lie I had told. As soon as the coast was clear, I opened my locker again.

Pinocula tried to comfort me by admitting he said a lot of things that he shouldn't.

IT'S A PUPPET CONDITION. MAYBE YOU JUST NEED A CRICKET, OR A CONSCIENCE.

My body began to ache and my eyes burned as I walked with Pinocula down the hall and out to the bus. I was glad my closet had created something new, but I was beginning to worry that Pinocula was making my life much more confusing than it needed to be.

WHAT'S THAT A PAINTING OF?

MY LIFE.

CHAPTER 5

FINDING THE BOOKS

Before I got home I put Pinocula in my backpack so that my mom wouldn't see him. I felt pretty certain she'd know Pinocula wasn't a cousin of mine.

HE'S YOUR SISTER'S KID.

REALLY? I DON'T REMEMBER HIM.

THAT PROBABLY MAKES HIM FEEL BAD.

There were a lot of things running around in my brain at the moment. The loudest thought in my head had to do with me finding the books I needed to read so that I would better understand Pinocula. The school library didn't have the books, and the public library wouldn't let me visit at the moment—I guess they were still bothered by the fort that Jack and I had built out of books last time we were there. The books I needed were probably in my closet, seeing how they had helped bring Pinocula to life, but my closet was locked. I had learned from experience that if Beardy didn't want to open up, there was no way we could bust it open.

Pinocula wanted to lie down and think, so I put him in the bottom drawer of my dresser. It had worked for Hairy, but it seemed more fitting for Pinocula.

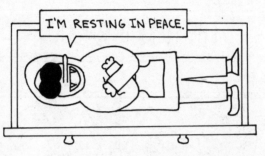

With Pinocula comfortable, I slipped out my window and headed to the rock island to hang with my friends and see if by some chance they had any books.

The island was in the middle of our cul-de-sac. It was covered with rocks and had a couple patches of grass, a dozen bushes, and a few palm trees. It was the perfect place to hang out.

THE NEIGHBORHOOD + SPOTS OF INTEREST

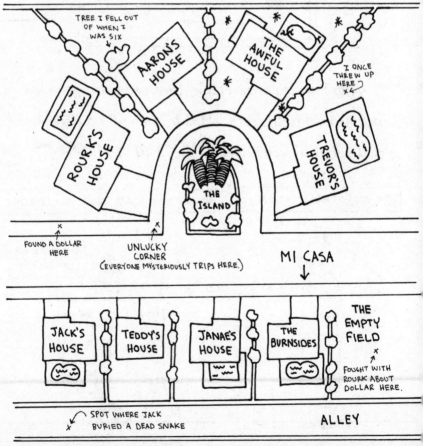

The only person on the island at the moment was Trevor. He had his model wolf and was building a fort for it.

Trevor always got into whatever he was studying. It didn't matter how stupid or boring the subject was. His last school project had been one of his most embarrassing.

I told him that I also liked wolves, but that I had
more important things on my mind.

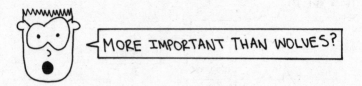

MORE IMPORTANT THAN WOLVES?

I took a few minutes to fill Trevor in. At first, he
was confused because he still thought Pinocula was my
cousin. After a little more explaining, he understood
that Pinocula was a new creature from my closet.
He got extra pumped when he remembered that
vampires and wolves go together.

KEN & LARRY'S KEN & LARRY'S KEN
VAMPIRE
AND
WOLF
FLAVORED ICE CREAM
TWO GROSS TASTES THAT TASTE
GROSS TOGETHER!

Trevor suggested we go to his house. His mom was heavily into vampire books and movies, and he thought she might have a copy of *Dracula*. It was strange to me that Trevor's mom liked vampires. She was known for being scared of the dark and against any books that had questionable and grown-up words in them. But according to Trevor she had no problem with glittery vampires.

Trevor's mom wasn't home, so we went to her bookshelf and searched for ourselves. There, in the middle of the bottom shelf, was the book I'd been looking for.

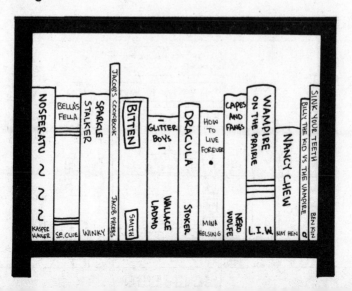

Trevor pulled out *Dracula* and told me I could borrow it. He said his mom didn't like *Dracula* as much as the other books because there were no handsome vampires in it. They didn't have a copy of *Pinocchio*. Trevor suggested we check with Mr. Harker who lived a few streets over. Mr. Harker and his wife were constantly trying to get people to join their book club. They also liked to brag about how many books they owned, so there was a good chance they'd have a copy of *Pinocchio*.

Trevor and I walked through the alley behind my house and down through another alley to get to the Harkers' house. When we finally got there, I was a little reluctant to knock.

I finally got up the courage and rang the doorbell. Mr. and Mrs. Harker answered together. They looked like they had been standing right behind the door waiting for someone to ring.

They were super pumped to see two young minds looking for books. When I asked them if they had a copy of *Pinocchio*, Mr. Harker said,

Mr. Harker went on and on about how much he had loved the book *Pinocchio* as a child. He also informed us that his book club would be meeting tomorrow evening and he thought it might be fun to do a reading.

DOESN'T THAT SOUND LIKE FUN?

WE'LL READ THE WHOLE BOOK OUT LOUD AS A GROUP.

I HAVE NO IDEA.

I'M STILL NOT SURE.

Before we could leave his house, I had to promise that I'd come back for the reading tomorrow. Mr. Harker also kept the copy of *Pinocchio* to have it waiting for me.

While we were walking home, Trevor and I tried to figure out what had just happened. We were both a little confused.

When we got back to my house, I took Trevor to my room to show him my new creature. I wanted to talk to Pinocula about a bunch of stuff, but he was still resting.

I closed the drawer. Trevor was pretty disappointed that Pinocula wasn't in the mood to talk.

Trevor went home, and I got down to the business of reading *Dracula*. The book was a struggle to get into at first. When I read *Harry Potter* and *Star Wars*, they felt new and futuristic. *Dracula* seemed like a story really old people would like.

I SAY, THIS HAS ALL THE TRAPPINGS OF A FIRST-RATE ADVENTURE.

I DECLARE.

The book began with a man going to Transylvania to help Dracula buy a house. Most of it was written in letters or journal entries, sort of like the book you are holding right now. The difference is I'm writing and drawing The Creature from My Closet books so that future generations will know what happens behind my odd closet door. I think the author of *Dracula* was just writing to scare people.

When dinnertime came, I skipped it so I could keep reading. The book was really beginning to grow on me.

I started to feel like I was in it and I was the one
writing the letters and having to save the world
from Dracula. The book even talked about wolves a
few times. I couldn't wait to tell Trevor. When I was
about halfway finished, I decided I'd better go to
sleep. It was only eight o'clock, but I was pooped.
As I was shutting the book, the bottom drawer of
my dresser slid open, and Pinocula sat up and
stretched.

I pleaded with Pinocula to keep resting, but he wanted no part of that. It was dark, and he was itching to do something. I tried to grab him, but he jumped up to the window, slid it open, and sprang out. I climbed out after him, begging him to stop. It was night, but there was still enough moonlight to see.

Pinocula reached the island. He hopped onto one of the large rocks and looked around. I was just about to lecture him on the importance of doing what I said when something near the palm trees made a noise. I grabbed Pinocula and held him behind me. Then "something" stepped out from the trees.

Jack was out on the island by himself, standing between the palm trees, doing nothing. Pinocula started talking, and because he was behind my back, it looked like I was speaking.

I'M A REAL BOY.

Jack stared at me for a few seconds. I think he was trying to decide if he still wanted to be friends. He tried to look behind my back, but I kept moving to keep Pinocula hidden. At first he wondered if I was holding my cousin, but then he realized ...

Reluctantly, I pulled Pinocula out from behind my back. It was dark, but Jack could see enough of him to guess what he was.

I was going to lecture Jack on keeping Pinocula a secret when I suddenly felt weak. My thumb where I had been bitten began to tingle. I rocked back and forth.

I fell to the ground before I finished my thought.

CHAPTER 6

ABANDONED

I know that part of the reason I am writing all of this is because someday it might *be* important to the scientific community.

NEXT TO WATER, WE HAVE DISCOVERED NOTHING MORE IMPORTANT THAN THE WRITINGS AND DRAWINGS OF ROB.

Because of that I should probably include a few scientific facts. Here's one. Being bitten by a weird batlike creature that comes out of your closet can be hazardous to your health. One moment I was standing on the island talking to Jack and holding Pinocula, and the next thing I know I'm lying on the floor in a dark room. I could hear Jack and Pinocula saying stupid things about me.

MAYBE HIS SPINE LIQUEFIED AND HE CAN NO LONGER STAND.

MAYBE WE SHOULD BURY HIM. THAT ALWAYS HELPS ME.

I sat up and they jumped back. Both of them were wearing glow bracelets that they must have gone and taken out of my room.

I was surprised to see Trevor. Jack let me know
that he and Pinocula had run into Trevor while they
were dragging me to the Awful House. Trevor
had been outside letting his model wolf look at
the moon.

BASK IN THE
LIGHT, FRIEND.

Taking me to the Awful House had been Pinocula's
idea. The place was empty, and the front door had
been left open. He also felt the home had terrific
curb appeal.

I sat up all the way and looked around. Pinocula cleared his throat and told us the real reason he had come into the Awful House was that he believed the bat thing that was once under his hat was now in here. His nose and fangs grew a little as he spoke. I asked him how he knew the bat was in here, and he told me he'd received a telegraph telling him. When I informed him that there were no telegraphs in use around here, he said,

IT CAME BY A RIDER ON HORSEBACK.

I explained to Pinocula that most information was not delivered by horse these days and that he might want to ease up on the lying. His nose was longer than ever now.

WHY?

Pinocula decided to give me some truth, and as he did, his nose and teeth started to shrink. He told me that this really did *seem* like a place his batty friend would like. He added that if the bat had bitten me, we needed to find him in order to save my life. I set Pinocula up on the windowsill to talk seriously with him. He took off his glasses for a moment so that we would be more eye to eye.

We began to search the abandoned Awful House to check for the bat. It wasn't easy to see anything because our glow bands weren't very bright. We crept down the hallway and toward the kitchen. Jack was right behind me, and Pinocula was hanging from my right arm. The kitchen door was open just a crack. When I pushed on it, it clicked and a low growl sounded from behind it.

The growling got louder and angrier. We spun around and ran as a large dog burst out of the kitchen and chased after us. We jammed through the front door. Jack took off toward his house, and Trevor whipped off toward his while I carried Pinocula and dashed toward mine. I was hoping that Jack smelled the tastiest so that the dog would chase after him. It was a horrible thing to think.

Luckily, the dog didn't chase after any of us. Pinocula and I made it across the street and climbed back into my window. We crashed down onto my bedroom floor. As I tried to catch my breath, Pinocula kept talking about the Awful House and how homey it was. He had particularly enjoyed the wolf. I tried to explain to him that it was just a neighborhood dog who was sniffing around the abandoned Awful House. I also explained that he needed to stay in my room.

I reminded Pinocula that he might not have any strings, but he did have me. So I gently picked him up, put him in his drawer, and closed it. I then duct-taped my drawer to make sure he stayed put.

I knew it was foolish to put him in my drawer and think everything was going to be okay, but I was exhausted. It seemed to me that a good night's sleep might be just what I needed. I was too tired to count whole fried chickens like my dad always suggested. So I settled for counting small chicken nuggets jumping into their box. I didn't make it past five.

CHAPTER 7

~

GLASSES HALF-FOOL

Falling asleep may have been easy, but waking up was hard. It was so bright outside, and the light coming through my window roughed me up like some sort of sun bully.

WHY ARE YOU WARMING YOURSELF? HUH? HUH?

I got out of bed and closed my curtains. I looked down at my dresser and realized that my morning wasn't going to be getting better anytime soon. Pinocula had chewed his way out of my drawer.

I gazed around my room, but he was nowhere. I opened my curtains and looked out. There was no sign of Pinocula. I searched the landscape, but he was harder to spot than the time I had lost Tuffin at the Thumb Buddies Festival.

The sky was tremendously bright. I closed the
curtains and started to get ready for school. My dad
must have just put new lightbulbs in the bathroom
because when I went to take a shower it was way
too lit up. So I left the lights off and showered in
the dark.

After the shower I went to the kitchen to eat breakfast and worry about Pinocula. Tuffin was in the kitchen with Puck. He was filling a small plastic bag with cold oatmeal.

Tuffin always makes food in the morning that he eats later in the day. Oatmeal was not the smartest choice, but it was better than when he used to store big wads of wet scrambled eggs between the couch cushions. I'll never forget the day Trevor accidentally found out about that.

UM, MY PANTS ARE WET.

I HOPE YOU LIKE EGGS.

This morning I didn't care what Tuffin was making. All I cared about was my eyes. It felt like they were on fire.

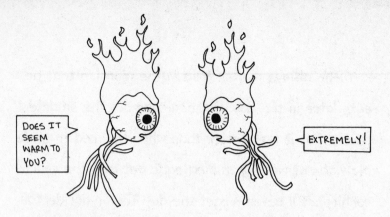

The only *sunglasses* I found in the house were an old pair that my dad had gotten at a rock concert years ago. They looked horrible, but they made my eyes feel much better. My dad came into the kitchen to have the two prunes and half a cup of milk he ate every morning. He saw me wearing his old glasses.

My dad thought *sick* was just another way for kids to say *cool*. So he patted me on the back and told me to have a great day.

I ate some cereal and slipped out of the house and over to my bus stop to wait for the bus. When I got there, Teddy, Rourk, and Aaron were surprised to see me wearing glasses.

Janae walked over and commented on my glasses being retro. She also wanted to know if I was serious

about the limo. I was going to tell her the truth,
but I didn't.

Aaron and Rourk didn't believe me. They began to
give me grief and ask why I had never mentioned
the limousine before. I began to lie some more.

Everyone was thrilled about that. They kept asking me questions, and the lies just kept pouring out of my mouth. With every lie my swollen nose hurt more and more.

I told them that the news was going to hide cameras at our school because they wanted to film a real middle school dance. I told them the limo fits twelve and that it used to belong to a movie star. I also told them that there would be hidden cameras everywhere. After I had lied enough for an entire lifetime, Rourk raised his hand and asked,

UM, WILL THERE BE ANY HIDDEN CAMERAS IN THE BATHROOMS?

By the time we got to Softrock Middle School, the entire bus was buzzing about the limo and the secret cameras. All day long, kids kept coming up to me begging me to let them ride in the limo. Jocks, rockers, goths, cheerleaders, cowboys, even one of the math club geeks.

LOOK, YOU LEAVE YOUR HOUSE IN A LIMO THAT HAS TWELVE SPOTS. YOU HAVE FIVE FRIENDS PLUS ONE—YOU—THAT EQUALS SIX. ADD THE THREE FEMALES YOU ARE INCLUDING AND YOU STILL HAVE A SURPLUS OF THREE. THREE MINUS ONE—ME—STILL LEAVES YOU WITH A REMAINDER OF TWO WHOLE SEATS.

Despite people bothering me, my mind was on Pinocula. He had made it to school yesterday, so I assumed he'd show up today. My teachers were also curious about where my cousin was.

In my last class, Janae kept turning around and talking to me. Apparently all a guy needs to do to be popular is to lie about having a limo and secret news coverage. Janae wanted to know what news station was doing the secret story. She wanted to know who the movie star was that had once ridden in the limo. I begged my brain to tell her the truth. It'd be embarrassing, but not as embarrassing as showing up the night of the dance with no limo and having to take her to the dance in Tuffin's wagon.

MY LADY.

I knew the only reason Janae was going to the dance with me was because I had lied. I just wasn't brave enough to set things straight. Overly friendly Todd leaned over from his desk and interrupted my conversation with Janae.

HEY, FRIEND. IF YOU HAVE TWO EXTRA SEATS IN THAT LIMO, COUNT ME IN!

WELL, MY MOM NEEDS A SPOT.

YOU TAKE UP TWO SEATS?

At the end of the day, Principal Smelt stopped me in the hall. He wanted me to take off my glasses. I couldn't think of a good excuse to keep them on so I told him . . .

Principal Smelt asked me if there was room in the limo for him. I told him no, and he tried to act like it was no big deal by whistling loudly and walking off. This limo thing was going to be the death of me. I needed to get things in order. I needed to stop messing around and finally devour the books *Pinocchio* and *Dracula* so I could figure out how to deal with Pinocula.

CHAPTER 8

THE READ ALOUD

As soon as I got home I searched my house for
Pinocula. No luck. I was going to climb out my
window into the bright outdoors when my mom called.

RIBERT.

I walked to the kitchen, where she was holding a piece of fancy paper with a tiny ribbon at the top. She looked confused and handed it to me.

I had forgotten about the *book club*. I had promised the Harkers that I'd go, but it looked like I was being used to advertise the event. My mom wanted some answers. I told her that Trevor and I had agreed to go to the *book club* because we were reading a ton lately.

My mom *shook* her head *slowly*, like she did when I brought home my report card or after one of my friends had belched really loud. She wanted me to take off the sunglasses, but I told her it was my thing. She also wanted me to play with Tuffin, but I let her know that wasn't my thing.

As soon as she got done talking at me, I ran over to Trevor's house. I found Trevor, and the two of us went to the Awful House. Pinocula had been so interested in the Awful House, I figured it'd be a good place to start looking for him. We slowly walked up the cracked sidewalk to the front door and knocked like we were two salesmen selling vacuums. Then I heard someone yell, "Coming!"

The door opened and there was Pinocula.

It was dark and cool inside the Awful House. There was an empty cardboard box standing against the corner that Pinocula must have dragged in from the alley. Scattered all over the floor were a bunch of sticks and logs.

Pinocula explained that he had fallen in love with the Awful House last night and that he wished to purchase it. I guess, like the real Dracula, Pinocula wanted to buy a place of his own. When I tried to explain that he didn't have any money, he started talking about how he was a real boy and how he had the right to a real house. Trevor had a few things to say about that.

THIS IS REAL DUMB. IT'S ALSO REAL TRESPASSING.

I argued with Pinocula, but he insisted he had already paid for the house and had permission to live here. Each lie he told made his nose grow.

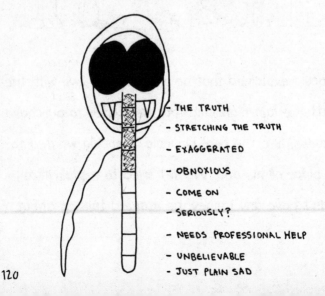

- THE TRUTH
- STRETCHING THE TRUTH
- EXAGGERATED
- OBNOXIOUS
- COME ON
- SERIOUSLY?
- NEEDS PROFESSIONAL HELP
- UNBELIEVABLE
- JUST PLAIN SAD

It was easy to see how stupid Pinocula's lies were, and that made me feel even worse about mine. As I was feeling bad about myself, I noticed Pinocula pacing around the room. He was walking strangely. His right leg was dragging, and his left foot clicked against the floor with each step. I knelt down by him.

I picked Pinocula up and took a better look at him. Unlike before, both his arms now felt wooden. When

I touched his ear, it also seemed woody. I couldn't tell for sure, but it looked as if the Pinocchio part of him was taking over the vampire part.

I THINK YOU'RE TURNING INTO ALL WOOD.

IT SEEMS AS IF THE UN-DEAD PART OF ME IS BEING SMOTHERED BY THE PUPPET PART. I MIGHT NEED TO BE BURIED FOR A WHILE TO GET BETTER.

It was one thing for a vampire to be un-dead, but it was another thing for a puppet to be. An un-dead puppet was just a piece of wood. If Pinocula continued changing, he'd be nothing but a lifeless doll by the end of the week. Trevor pointed out that I didn't look that great either. Trevor said I seemed pale and that my hair was getting darker. I didn't want to tell Trevor, but ever since I had been bitten by that bat thing, I hadn't felt well. I was glad I was going to the book club tonight. With any luck I'd learn what I needed to about Pinocchio and my condition. As for *Dracula*, it was important to finish that book, too. I had about an hour before the book club to read, but I knew that if I went home my mom would just make me watch Tuffin or do chores. I turned and looked at Trevor. I believe he saw the urgency written all over my face.

GET ME THAT BOOK!

Trevor raced from the Awful House and back to my home to retrieve *Dracula*. He popped through my window, found the book, and was back in less than a minute. I took the book and picked up where I left off. Pinocula rested in his box near me and Trevor sat on the floor while I read by the light of the gloom.

IS IT DARK ENOUGH FOR YOU?

YES.

READ THAT PART ABOUT THE WOLVES AGAIN.

We read until a few minutes before five. At that point, Trevor and I went to my house to tell my mom we were going to the book club. My mom insisted we take Tuffin with us because I had been out of the house and had missed valuable time with my brother.

Tuffin was happy to be included and way more excited about going to a book club than anyone should ever be.

BOOKS, BOOKS, BOOKS, PAGES!

We took the alleys to the Harkers' house and were there in no time. I was wearing my backpack with Pinocula packed comfortably inside. He said he really liked how dark it was. I had thought about leaving him in the Awful House, but I figured it might be a good idea for him to hear the story of Pinocchio. We knocked on the door, and when it opened, it was obvious from the way the Harkers were dressed that they were really getting into this book club reading.

I thought it would just be the Harkers and a couple other old people at the book club, but the room was filled with kids. Even Jack and Teddy were there. They had all gotten flyers, and they wanted to come so that they could observe me in my book club environment.

We all sat in a big circle on a bunch of mismatched stools. I sat in the darkest corner so that the light wouldn't make me sick. Mrs. Harker passed out the books while Mr. Harker explained that we'd be taking turns reading and that we should prepare our minds for adventure. I was glad to see that the book wasn't very thick.

THICKNESS METER

UNCLE PHIL

PIECE OF PAPER

PINOCCHIO

PHONE BOOK

NOT THICK   SLIM   THINNISH   THICK   THICKER   THICKER STILL   BEYOND THICK   CONCERNING

The reading went way better than I thought it would. Everyone read a part, and the story was both odd and interesting. I really identified with bits of Pinocula's personality that had come from the wooden puppet. Trevor said he liked the beginning of the story, but he felt it lacked wolves.

Mr. Harker did most of the reading. While he read, Pinocula squirmed and wiggled in my backpack. His woody elbows and knees kept jabbing me in my back and made me look way more into the story than I was.

PINOCCHI-OW!

GEPPETT-OW!

In the book, Geppetto was mean at the start and Pinocchio was a smart aleck who wore a hat made of dough and shoes made from bark. He was also friends with a bunch of talking dogs and mice and blue-haired fairies and donkeys. Plus he smashed a talking cricket with a hammer. I don't remember ever seeing that in the Disney version. He also made a bunch of bad decisions and got into some real trouble. I was wondering if Pinocula was listening in my backpack, but when Mr. Harker read a part where Pinocchio was thrown into the sea to die, Pinocula cried out sadly.

I had to pretend that it was me who had screamed. Mr. Harker was touched that his reading was so powerful it had caused me to get emotional. As he began to read again, something loud thumped against the window near me. Mr. Harker stopped reading, and we all looked toward the window. Mr. Harker pulled back the curtains, but the only thing there was the newly dark night.

He closed the curtain again and cleared his throat in preparation to read. Before he could get a word out, another thump sounded. Mr. Harker spun and pulled the curtains open. He threw open the window, leaned out, and yelled,

IF IT'S YOU SMITH BOYS AGAIN, I'M CALLING THE COPS.

Nothing but a cool breeze drifted back. Before Mr. Harker could close the window, something black darted in and swooped directly toward me. I barely had time to freak out. I might even have used one of Rourk's made-up swear words.

MOLDY SHIP!

Pinocula's cry had summoned the bat I had been looking for. I swatted it with my hands while Pinocula hollered and laughed in my backpack. Tuffin thought it was all a big game and started to clap and dance in a circle. Everyone else began to swat at their heads. Mr. Harker sprang into action. He pulled off his shirt and caught the bat in it like a net.

I'VE CAUGHT THE BUGGER!

Pinocula began to violently thrash in my backpack. I pulled off my pack and tried to hold it still. Pinocula pushed his face out of a corner of the zipper.

I guess the bat's name was Jim. I ran after Mr. Harker who was storming toward the front door with the shirt-net. I begged him not to hurt Jim, and he turned around in surprise. The entire book club froze and looked at me.

Tuffin was happy about my new lie. Mr. Harker was happy we brought a pet, but his wife wished we had brought a different one. Mrs. Harker got a small, pink plastic sandwich container, carefully put Jim inside, and sealed it up. Mr. Harker poked some tiny holes in the top and handed it to Tuffin.

HERE'S YOUR PET.

Mrs. Harker insisted that Jim be put out on the porch while we finished the story. I wanted to leave then, but I knew I needed to hear the end of the book, and I for sure didn't want to come back some other time. I took the container and put it out on the porch while everyone returned to their seats. The rest of the book was interesting, but I was distracted by the fact that Jim was out front. I got to read the part where Pinocchio was turned into a donkey and where he and Geppetto were swallowed by a mile-long shark. Trevor read the part at the end when Pinocchio finally got what he wanted.

It had taken a little over two hours to read the whole book. When we were done, Mr. Harker suggested that the group stay and watch the Disney movie of *Pinocchio* to see how different or similar it was to the book. Teddy had another suggestion.

People started to leave, and Tuffin began to talk about Jim. He was so hyped to have a new pet. I didn't have the heart to tell Tuffin he wouldn't be able to keep him. The second we left, I was going to send Tuffin home with Trevor and take Jim to the Awful House to see if he could help me and Pinocula figure out what was wrong with me. As we were leaving, I picked up the pink bat container from the porch and thanked the Harkers.

I tried to get them to let us just walk home, but they wouldn't take no for an answer. So we all got into the Harkers' station wagon, and he drove us to my house. Mr. Harker sang embarrassing songs while he drove.

Tuffin carried the pink container on his lap. He kept saying "Jim" over and over while I kept wondering how I was going to explain a pet bat to my parents.

I was pretty sure my mom wasn't going to buy it.

CHAPTER 9

SURPRISE!

Here's the thing about parents—just when you think
you have them figured out, they go and do something
that surprises the heck out of you.

I thought my mom would freak out about Tuffin having a bat. I thought there'd be scolding and punishments and demands to get rid of the bat. Instead she said,

I ALWAYS THOUGHT BATS WERE SORT OF CUTE. I THINK WE HAVE AN OLD TERRARIUM WE CAN KEEP IT IN.

My dad was also highly pleased. He said we could keep the bat for a few days before we let it go. But he added,

THOSE FEW DAYS WILL BE SOME OF THE FINEST WE'VE EVER HAD!

I don't know what my dad thought bats were capable of, but personally I felt like he was promising more than the bat was capable of delivering. Libby acted just like I thought she would.

I WILL NOT SHARE A HOUSE WITH SUCH AN UGLY CREATURE. I ALREADY HAVE TO SHARE IT WITH ROB.

My dad got our old terrarium down from the attic and cleaned it out. He put a little stick and a dish of water in it. Then he carefully emptied the container with the bat inside and closed the top. Looking through the glass, I saw that the poor creature had its wings wrapped around its head and was balled up in the corner. None of us were able to get a good look at him. I needed everyone to go to bed so I could sneak out and take Jim away.

I should have known my dad would say that. If our water heater wasn't working, my dad slept next to it to hear what sounds it was making. If Puck was acting sick, he would curl up next to him and evaluate his breathing all night long, and if the car wasn't working, he would sleep in the back seat and listen for weird noises. It never really fixed anything, but my dad claimed it helped clear his head and give him a better understanding of the problem. Now the new bat was here, and he and Tuffin were going to make their beds next to it. My father and brother quickly changed and got sleeping bags.

I left my father and the terrarium for a moment and went to check on Pinocula. I had hidden him under my bed when I got home from the book club, and I was hoping he had stayed put for once. I should have been tired but I wasn't. I was feeling stronger now. I moved quickly to my room and shut my bedroom door. Pinocula looked at me and smiled weakly. I pulled him out and studied him a bit closer. He was barely moving.

His nose grew at least three inches. He looked paler and woodier than ever. I was more than just a little worried.

Pinocula wanted to be back at the Awful House. He liked how unfinished and run-down it was. I suggested he stay with me, but he really wanted to rest there. He seemed so pitiful that I couldn't resist helping him. I carried Pinocula out the window and over to the Awful House. He perked up a little when I laid him back down in his cardboard box that he had filled with dirt.

I was glad Pinocula thought something felt right, because something felt wrong with me. I was beginning to feel more and more like someone else. I liked the dark and I didn't feel like sleeping. That bat bite had done me wrong.

Pinocula closed his eyes and began to talk. As he talked his nose grew smaller, letting me know he was telling the truth. He told me that the night usually made him stronger, but tonight he felt weaker than ever. He believed that as the puppet part of him smothered the vampire part, he would perish and move from un-dead to just dead. He also instructed me that when that happened he needed to be buried under at least a foot of soil as soon as possible. He also believed that when he passed on I'd return to my normal self. I couldn't let him die. The little guy had grown on me.

Pinocula closed his eyes and rested. It was unsettling seeing him sleep in the dark. He was usually so alive and obnoxious at night. As much as I wanted to stay near him, I knew I needed to get back home to keep an eye on Jim. I didn't want Tuffin or my dad to accidentally harm him in any way. I picked up the Dracula book and left Pinocula to rest. When I got home I sat on a chair near Jim and my sleeping father and brother and read for the rest of the night. I never got tired, but I did get creeped out by the story. It was scarier than my dad's snoring.

When I finished the book it was 6:30 in the morning. It was also now the day of the dance. I really loved the book, but I felt pretty certain that I never wanted to be a vampire. The ending was cool, but it didn't exactly turn out great for Count Dracula.

LISTEN, I'LL LOAN YOU THE BOOK, BUT I GUARANTEE YOU'RE NOT GOING TO LIKE THE ENDING.

As I thought about it, though, I wasn't sure what was worse—death or the dance tonight. I had no limo, there wouldn't be a secret news crew, and I was about to let down a ton of people I liked.

I got up from the chair and found a phone book. I had forty dollars saved in my piggy bank. I figured if I found a cheap limo to rent maybe I could fix one of my lies.

150

There were a few options to call, but none of the limo places were open this early. I tore the page out of the phone book and put it in my wallet. I quickly took a shower and got ready for school. When I was dressed, I headed to the kitchen to get something to eat and check on Jim. I was surprised to find my mom sitting alone by the terrarium staring at him. She was in her robe and squinting, trying to get a good look.

My mom tilted her head and attempted to look at the head and body of Jim. She shifted the terrarium and gazed at the bat from another angle. I tried to make myself breakfast without looking suspicious. I poured a big bowl of my favorite cereal and sat down at the table.

My mom was tapping the glass and talking to Jim. I started to wonder if Jim had the ability to speak. It wasn't normal for bats to say things, but it also wasn't normal for creatures to come out of people's closets. I'd be in a ton more trouble if Jim suddenly started talking. I needed to get my mom's mind off the bat fast. I brought up the one subject I thought might interest her.

I'M GOING TO NEED SOMETHING TO WEAR TO THE DANCE TONIGHT.

I don't know how normal kids tell their parents things, but apparently I do it the wrong way. I'm not sure why she needed to know that I was going to the dance any sooner than now. I figured a ten-hour notice was enough. My mom stood up and started rubbing her forehead.

Apparently, my family doesn't keep extra tuxes on hand. My mom looked torn—one half of her looked like it wanted to be mad at me while the other half looked like it was thrilled to know I was going to a dance.

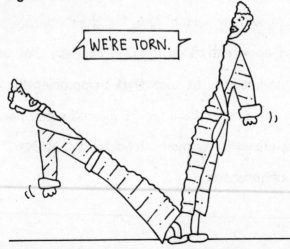

My mom rubbed her forehead some more. She was upset, but she promised she'd find something for me to wear after she took Jim to Tuffin's school for show-and-tell.

I couldn't let Jim go to Tuffin's school. My dad came into the kitchen dressed and set for the day. He told my mom he'd take over bat duty so she would be able to get ready.

IF THERE'S A PROBLEM I'LL FLASH YOU THE BAT SIGNAL.

There was a problem, but my dad just wasn't aware of it. The problem was that if anyone at Tuffin's school noticed that Jim was more than just a bat, there might be real trouble. I had to fix this. My mom left to get ready for the day, leaving me alone with my father. Lying had become so easy for me lately that I went with it again.

NOW THAT IT'S DAYLIGHT WE NEED TO COVER THIS TERRARIUM.

REALLY?

YES, I LEARNED IN SCHOOL THAT BATS MUST HAVE DARKNESS DURING THE DAY OR THEY'LL SHRIVEL UP AND DIE.

THAT MAKES SENSE.

I got an old blanket, and we draped it over the terrarium. I told my dad we needed to tape the blanket so that it wouldn't come off. He headed to the garage to get some duct tape. The second he was gone I grabbed the pink sandwich container that Jim had originally been in. With one swift movement I pulled the blanket off, lifted the top of the terrarium, scooped up Jim into the container, and put on the lid. I looked around for something to put into the terrarium to take Jim's place. I saw the perfect object. I grabbed it and tossed it in. I put the top on and draped the blanket over the whole thing. I set the pink container with Jim in it on the counter.

I turned around just as my dad walked in. He didn't see a thing. Together we wrapped duct tape around the terrarium.

Tuffin came into the kitchen and wanted to see Jim, but I told him that bats can die from being peeked at. I grabbed the pink container and ran to my room. I shoved it into my backpack and left. When I got to the Awful House, Pinocula was still in his box resting peacefully. He opened his eyes, but he looked less un-dead than ever. When I asked him if he could move he said,

OF COURSE. I JUST GOT DONE RUNNING A MARATHON.

Pinocula might have lacked the strength to walk, but he was still a really strong liar. I picked him up and he just hung there limply in my arms.

I THINK YOU'RE ALMOST COMPLETELY WOODEN.

I COULD USE SOME BOARDS TO CHEW ON.

Pinocula tried to swing his arm up in an attempt to nibble on it, but he was too weak. I picked up a stick lying on the ground and held it close to his mouth for him. I thought about the books *Dracula* and *Pinocchio*. Both books had been good, but I couldn't see how either one could help me now. I remembered Jim. I ripped off my backpack and pulled out the pink container. When I opened it I gasped.

I didn't have Jim. I had Libby's lunch! She had packed hers in a pink container that looked just like the one I used. I put Pinocula into my backpack and tore out of the Awful House and back to mine. When I got into the kitchen there was nobody there. There was also nothing on the counter. I looked around. The terrarium was gone. I checked Libby's room and she wasn't there. I looked out in the garage and the cars were missing. I had been away only a few minutes, but in that time my whole family had left. This was not a good morning. Pinocula was getting weaker, Jim was missing, and my gut hurt from all the lies I was trying to remember. I wanted to remove my stomach, heart, and all my insides that were currently bringing me down.

Unfortunately, my insides were still right where they should be, which meant I felt as bad as I should.

CHAPTER 10

—

LIMO AND LIES

I barely made it to my school bus on time. It was
an uncomfortable ride—Pinocula felt bulky in my
backpack, and everyone was talking about the
dance tonight and what they were going to wear.
Janae sat across from me in the aisle and asked
me if I was going to wear my sunglasses forever. I
nodded. The light still hurt my eyes. She wanted to
know what time I'd be picking her up for the dance.
It was now or never. If I told her the truth, she

would probably just not like me, which wouldn't be that unusual. I looked Janae in her blue eyes, cleared my throat, and said,

I'LL PICK YOU UP AT SIX.

Janae turned to talk and plan with her friends. Everyone kept patting me on the shoulder and thanking me for bringing the news crew to our school. They also kept telling me how lucky I was to be going to the dance in a limo. I didn't feel lucky, and when I got to school, I was so out of sorts I felt like I had been put together wrong.

I stashed Pinocula in my locker and tried to just
get through the day. The world seemed topsy-turvy.
I was sick of what I had become. It seemed as
if I were turning into Aaron. Aaron had always
struggled with telling the truth. Almost everything
he said was a lie.

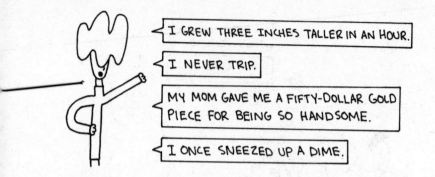

Now I was worse than he was. Usually the school day dragged on, but today time flew. Every minute that slipped away I knew I was getting closer to the dance and closer to being busted. I checked on Pinocula between classes. He would just blink at me and make up some sort of lie.

After school, I went straight to the Awful House with Jack and Pinocula. The plan was to leave Pinocula there tonight. Jack didn't want anything to do with a secret news crew, and he didn't care for dances. According to him,

DANCES ARE STUPID.

So I figured I'd let Jack keep an eye on Pinocula while I was gone. He was more than willing to do it. To him the thought of hanging out in an abandoned house and babysitting a vampire puppet was much less lame than dancing. After I got Pinocula and Jack situated, I headed home. The dance started in

less than two hours, and I still hadn't come up with
a lie to get out of all my other lies.

| ~~THE DANCE WAS CANCELLED DUE TO RAIN~~ |
| ~~DANCING HAS BEEN OUTLAWED~~ |
| ~~I CAN'T GO BECAUSE I HAVE MONO~~ |
| ~~I HAVE REALLY BAD STOMACH CRAMPS~~ |
| ~~THE LIMO EXPLODED~~ |
| ~~I NEED TO STAY NEAR A TOILET~~ |

When I got to my house, my mom was waiting
for me at the door. I could tell by the way she was
standing that I was in trouble.

My mom told me anyway. According to her, she had

placed the terrarium on a table in front of Tuffin's

class. She told all the kids there was a bat inside,

but when she took off the blanket, there was no bat.

I tried to convince my mom that it must have

been a fruit bat. She wouldn't buy it. She also had

more to tell me. She got a call from Libby while

Libby was at school today.

It's nice that she keeps in touch.

My mom didn't appreciate my sarcasm. I guess Libby was eating lunch, and when she opened her sandwich container, a bat flew out.

Did someone film it?

Not only wasn't it captured on film, but Jim had gotten away. As my mom scolded me, a thought popped into my head. If I got in big enough trouble, she might make me stay home from the dance.

I didn't want my mom to think about this, but she kept thinking, and what she thought was that I had done the right thing by telling her the truth. She appreciated the honesty and then told me,

She wouldn't hear of it. My mom had already picked up something for me to wear, and she had cleaned out the station wagon so it wouldn't be a mess when she drove me and all my friends. As I was telling her that I no longer had any friends, the doorbell rang. My mom opened the door and my no-friend lie was ruined.

I sighed and realized that I wasn't going to get out of it that easy. My friends all followed me back to my room. It was funny to see them dressed up. I had never seen Rourk in nice pants. The ones he had on were way too small and gave him a massive wedgie. He kept trying to fix it by wiggling.

All my friends were fidgeting and trying to act brave about going to the dance. They kept asking me questions that I didn't know the answer to.

I wouldn't have smelled Rourk's breath if it was
the last puff of air in the world. Besides, the way
my stomach was turning, I felt pretty certain my
breath was worse.

I changed into the clothes my mom got for me,
but I couldn't tie my tie quite right.

I told my friends to wait in the living room, and I ran to use the phone we had in the kitchen. I needed to have a private conversation. I pulled out the phone book page from my wallet and called one of the limo places.

The limousine companies kept hanging up on me. The tenth one I called laughed at me and explained that limos were usually booked days in advance and cost hundreds of dollars. After he gave me the information, he hung up on me, too.

I was out of options. There was only one thing to do. I had to tell the truth—I hated all the lying. I wasn't like Pinocchio—I couldn't deal with the turmoil in my gut. I squared my shoulders and walked out to confess everything. As I stepped into the living room, however, I saw that everybody was excitedly staring out the window at something. I looked for myself. There, shimmering under the light of the setting sun, was a limousine.

My friends all started yelping and dancing. I didn't understand what was going on. There had obviously been a mistake and someone else's limo had come to the wrong address. I mean, you don't just lie about something and it comes true. We all ran out to get a better look. As I stepped up to the limo, the driver's door opened and my dad got out.

GOOD EVENING, SIR. I'LL BE YOUR DRIVER TONIGHT.

What was happening? My dad came around the car and opened the door. All my friends quickly climbed in, laughing and shoving each other. I just stood there dumbfounded. My dad saw my confused face and leaned down to whisper to me.

PRINCIPAL SMELT CALLED ME. I HAD NO IDEA I WAS SUPPOSED TO RENT YOU A LIMO. BESIDES, WE CAN'T HAVE YOU SHOWING UP IN AN OLD STATION WAGON WITH ALL THOSE HIDDEN CAMERAS THAT ARE GOING TO BE THERE. PRINCIPAL SMELT ALSO SAID YOU MIGHT NEED THIS.

My dad slipped something into my hand without showing it to me. I got into the limo and tried to smile. I looked at what he had slipped me.

EYE ZIT CREAM
CURES PIMPLES NEAR YOUR PEEPERS

I didn't know if I was more bothered by Principal Smelt giving me acne eye cream or by the fact that it had already been used.

My dad closed the car door as I slipped the tube into my pocket. Inside the limo there was plenty of room for all of us and any friends Janae was bringing. I looked out the window and saw my dad putting a big magnetic sign on the side of the limo and a flag on the roof.

I guess he was using the limo to help advertise his playground company.

My dad got into the front seat, and we pulled out of the driveway. He drove about ten feet and stopped in front of Janae's house. I got out and walked up the sidewalk. I honestly hadn't thought I'd make it this far. It was just now sinking in that I was really going to the dance with Janae. I rang the doorbell.

HI, ROB.

Janae looked nice, her hair was fancy, and she was smiling like she was pleased to see me. Her friends were already there. My mom had walked over from our house, and she and Janae's mom took just under a million pictures. We then got into the limo and drove to the dance while Tuffin waved good-bye.

It was fun in the limo, but it also reminded me in an uncomfortable way of the wagon full of kids in the book *Pinocchio* as they traveled to Toyland, right before they were all turned into donkeys.

I was going to my very first dance with Janae. I don't think I could have been any happier, more scared, confused, worried, or curious about how it would all turn out.

CHAPTER 11

ALWAYS LET YOUR CONSCIENCE BE YOUR GUIDE

At first, everyone tried to act all reserved and proper in the limo, but then Aaron opened the moon roof and began yelling stupid things out the top.

Teddy wondered if the secret news crew had put hidden cameras in the car, so he kept flexing his muscles and smiling at nothing. There was a radio in the back and I turned it on. We all sang and talked loudly. It was so much fun that I was almost able to stop thinking about all the lies I had told. I also put Jim out of my mind and tried not to worry about Jack looking after Pinocula, even though I knew Jack probably was an awful babysitter.

TAKE THIS SPOONFUL OF KETCHUP AND THEN SOAK YOUR FEET IN THIS BOILING POT OF WATER. YOU'LL FEEL LIKE A NEW MAN? VAMPIRE? PUPPET? WHATEVER.

The parking lot of Softrock Middle School was filled with cars. Word had spread about the news crew and their hidden cameras. When our limo pulled in, people stared and pointed like we were stars arriving at a show. I had never seen Janae and her friends so happy. My friends were happy too, but they expressed it differently.

We walked into the school as a large group. The school had gone all out with the decorations. The doorway to the gym was a big whale's mouth that everyone walked through.

As I stepped into the mouth, I got a sinking feeling. I felt like Pinocchio as he was swallowed up by the giant mile-long shark. Janae and her friends walked off to talk with some of their other friends while we settled in by the punch bowl.

The room was decorated to make it look like we were under the sea, but some of the kids who had wanted a vampire theme had added their own touches to the decorations. There was a table with some food and a skinny kid with big earphones working as the DJ. The students had voted not to have Principal Smelt and his two-man rock group, Leftover Angst, play at the dance. Principal Smelt was still mad about it.

JOSEPH VAMPIRE 1862- ?

None of the students were dancing. Everyone was just lining the walls, trying to look and act cool in front of the hidden cameras that weren't there. The only people dancing were three teachers—two who were dancing together and a third who was humming and dancing by himself in an uncomfortable way.

Maggie, one of Janae's friends, came over to our group and stopped in front of me.

Maggie turned and walked away. All my friends stared at me as if I had just been told the most amazing thing in the world. I looked over at Janae, and she was pretending to be busy talking to someone. My tongue dried out and began to crack.

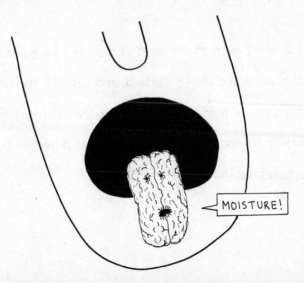

I looked down at my feet and wondered how I was still standing. It was one thing to come to a dance, but it was another thing altogether to actually dance. Teddy started chanting,

DO IT, DO IT, DO IT!

I looked over at Janae and decided to do what a real man would do—I turned and walked to the bathroom as quickly as possible. When I got there, I went into one of the stalls and sat down on top of the toilet to think.

I didn't feel right at all anymore. My eyes burned and the strength I had been feeling the day before was wearing off. How was I supposed to dance with Janae when I had never actually danced with a girl? Unless you count the time I had been forced to dance with my cousin Trish at our family reunion. But that was more like being carried around than dancing.

As I sat on top of the toilet, I heard something tapping against the window. I stood on the back of the toilet and looked up. I opened the window a little, and Jim fluttered right in. He glided down and landed on the roll of toilet paper. I was finally able to get a good look at him.

Jim was definitely half cricket, half bat. He had an interesting face and appeared to be looking right at me. I considered trying to catch him in my hands, but I didn't want to scare him. He winked at me and spoke.

HAVING A GOOD TIME, ROB? THERE'S NOTHING MORE MAGICAL THAN THE BATHROOM STALL.

Jim was a little more sarcastic than I had expected. I was going to defend my being in the bathroom, but he just kept talking.

DID THE NEWS CREW COME? YEAH, I DIDN'T THINK SO. YOU'VE MADE A MESS OF THINGS. YOU SHOULD KNOW LYING LEADS TO TROUBLE EVERY TIME.

YOU SHOULD KNOW YOU'RE PRETTY RUDE.

Jim was preachier than I preferred. He told me
that bad things were brewing and the only way to
stop them was for me to tell the truth.

Jim fluttered to the window. He looked back as if
he was going to leave. I jumped up and begged him
to stay.

Jim flew out the window and disappeared into the night. If he was supposed to be my conscience, he was the worst conscience ever. I now understood why Pinocula hadn't tried harder to find him. I hopped off the toilet and left the stall. I walked back into the dance, and stepped across the dance floor and up to Janae. She reached out, and without knowing what I was doing, I took her hand and we moved to the dance floor. There was music playing, our fingers were touching, and we were swaying.

Janae smiled and thanked me for coming to the dance with her. I opened my mouth to thank her, and she leaned in and kissed me on the cheek. I stumbled backward and suddenly became very light-headed.

My first kiss! Maybe all my lies were worth it. I mean, how bad can it be if this is the result? I'm sure I was about to do something smooth to let Janae know how I felt, but Jack ruined it all.

POP!

There he was, standing right next to me. Jack had crashed the dance and was holding what looked a little like Pinocula. Before I had a chance to tell him I had just been kissed and that he needed to leave, he spoke up.

Everyone gathered around noisily. Pinocula was no longer wearing the hoodie and pants. He looked wooden and was beginning to turn into a donkey. His legs and arms and ears hung down like pieces of wood. The DJ began to play some sort of polka song. Jack looked around at all the decorations and people.

Janae was curious about what Jack was holding.

Rourk answered her question.

Principal Smelt approached our group and looked at Jack and donkey Pinocula. He wasn't glad about Jack showing up with an odd puppet in his arms.

Principal Smelt took Jack by the arm and started to lead him away. Jack turned to say one last thing to me.

Principal Smelt and the rest of the students looked at Jack like he was crazy. Most of the students laughed, assuming that Jack was just being difficult like always. Principal Smelt scolded Jack for interrupting such a beautiful night with his made-up stories. He nudged Jack to get moving.

I heard myself say it, but I still wasn't sure why I had. Janae and my friends looked at me, curious to hear what I'd say next. I wanted to lie, I wanted to tell everyone that Jack collected donkey dolls and had brought this one to show it off to the hidden cameras. I wanted to tell them that I had done nothing wrong and that I had no idea what was going on, but I was done lying. I kept thinking of Jim and his warning. I turned and looked at Janae. I had just had my first kiss, and now I knew it would probably be my last. I took off my sunglasses and looked at her. My eyes didn't burn and things didn't seem quite as bright anymore. It was time to tell the truth.

Janae blushed slightly and stepped back. I had thought telling the truth was supposed to feel good, but I felt worse. Principal Smelt put his arm around me. He congratulated me on my eye acne clearing up and then commented on what I had just admitted.

Everyone began to holler and boo. A kid with head gear and thick corrective glasses called me a nerd. Janae turned away from me and slipped into a crowd of angry kids. The DJ began to play some sad music.

Principal Smelt looked bothered and confused. He stared at me and pointed across the room to a man with a small camera who appeared to be following us.

The man was a reporter who had come to film our dance because he was curious about the secret news cameras I had lied about. I didn't know what to think. I had lied about the limo, and one had shown up. I had lied about the cameras, and one had shown up. I should have lied about being stronger and better at playing sports. Principal Smelt looked at me and spoke.

I wanted to stay there and defend myself, but I needed to help Pinocula. I looked around for Jack, but he was already gone. I ran through the whale's mouth and out the front doors of the school. The dark sky was filled with stars. In the distance, I saw Jack carrying Pinocula and walking away. He was heading toward the park right across the street from our school. I ran up to him, and he turned to look at me.

I was going to apologize more, but there were no words that could correct what I'd done. I had messed up, and I'd have to pay for it. Trevor ran up to us. He had seen me run out and had chosen to follow.

I took Pinocula from Jack, and all of us ran to the park. I knew what we needed to do. We needed to return him to the soil.

For some reason Trevor and Jack kept running

with me.

CHAPTER 12

~

SOME BURIED PINOCULA

There was nobody in the park this late at night. Still, I wanted to make sure we found a good spot to bury my log-like friend. Pinocula was nothing but wood now. He looked like a donkey doll built out of wood. I knew he was no longer himself because I felt completely healed.

I was myself again, but I was very tired. All the sleep I had missed over the past week was trying to catch up to me.

I ran faster. I needed to bury Pinocula. I wasn't certain this would work, but it was what Pinocula had asked me to do.

We found a hidden spot behind a row of bushes where nobody ever walked. I dropped to my knees, set Pinocula on the ground, and told my friends to start digging. We started to dig with our hands, but the ground was hard and we weren't making much progress.

It was a great suggestion, but we didn't have a

shovel, and we didn't have time to go and get one.

According to Pinocula, he needed to be quickly buried

under a solid foot of soil to have any chance of

surviving. We all scratched at the ground violently. We

were so involved in what we were doing that we didn't

notice someone step up next to us and clear his throat.

I recognized the visitor immediately. It was Principal Smelt's second cousin, the city worker who had given the assembly that I had laughed at.

I was so juiced up on telling the truth that I just went for it.

The city worker stared at me. He looked at
Trevor and glanced at Jack. He took Pinocula from
Jack's arms and studied him closely.

He got his shovel, and after a while, we had a small
hole big enough for Pinocula. I laid him carefully in
the hole, and we pushed the dirt back over him.

We all thanked Principal Smelt's second cousin, and he walked off whistling with his shovel over his shoulder. Jack placed an old milk carton he found on the dirt as a headstone. We stood around the covered hole wondering what to do next.

I wanted to wait around to see if something would happen to Pinocula, but we heard a loud honking out in front of the school.

When we got a little closer, I saw that the person honking was my dad. He was blasting the horn of the long limousine. Everyone was leaving the dance, and I saw Janae and her friends getting back into the limo.

I wasn't going to show my face, so I sent Trevor to tell my dad that I had walked home because I needed to think about what I had done.

Jack and I took the alley and made our way to our houses. I felt horrible about leaving Pinocula. It was strange, though. I knew I was going to be in big trouble, but I felt a little lighter knowing I had finally told the truth. I figured I'd go home, get in trouble, and then tomorrow morning I'd come dig up Pinocula. It wasn't a great plan, but it was all I had at the moment.

Unfortunately, even un-great plans can experience great changes.

CHAPTER 13

—

TRANSFORMATIONS AND WELCOME GUESTS

I got in big trouble—huge trouble. I told my parents everything, and they didn't take it well. Mom was beyond mad about all my lies. She didn't know if she should wash my mouth out with soap or put me up for adoption. Libby suggested that she . . .

DO BOTH.

After the dance, my dad had driven everyone home and returned the limo. When he got back he was so disappointed in me, he almost looked mad.

I tried to tell them how sorry I was, but there weren't enough words in the English language to properly express myself.

LOSER SAD
PITIFUL SHOULDN'T HAVE
OOPS
GRIEVED BAD GUILT-RIDDEN
SORRY SORROWFUL
THE WORST APOLOGETIC LAME-O
CONTRITE LIED SCARED
I DIDN'T CONFUSED PATHETIC
DOOF-WADIOUS UNHAPPY VILE

When my parents were through lecturing me, they sent me to my room to think about what I had done. They also told me that I wasn't allowed to come out until they said so.

NOT EVEN TO USE THE BATHROOM!

I sat on the edge of my bed and sighed. I was so tired I thought I was going to just drop to the ground and start snoring. I stared in the mirror on my wall. I was surprised at how different I looked. My skin wasn't as pale, and my eyes were clearer. The experience of hanging out with Pinocula had been way different than hanging out with Hairy and Wonk. I needed a new closet.

I crawled into my bed, pulled up my blankets, and was out in two seconds flat.

In no time at all, the sun was up and someone was knocking at my window. I blinked rapidly and rubbed all the sleep out of my eyes. Someone knocked on my window again. I pulled the curtains open, and there was Trevor.

LOOK WHAT I FOUND SLEEPING OUT ON THE ISLAND.

Trevor was very pleased with his find. He had put a leash on the wolf. He also had his own theory about where the animal had come from.

I LEFT MY MODEL WOLF ON THE ISLAND AND LOOK WHAT IT'S TURNED INTO.

I knew Trevor was wrong. The animal he was holding had familiar eyes and the same hat as Pinocula. The wolf leapt up and jumped in through my window. Trevor crawled in after him. The beast began to shake and change its shape right in front of us.

In a few moments there was no sign of the wolf—only Pinocula, and he looked alive and strong. Plus, his arms and legs appeared to be real now. I knew from the book that vampires can shift their shapes, and Pinocula had just done a great job of it. Trevor looked a little disappointed, but I was relieved. The soil had revived Pinocula, and in the tradition of Dracula, he had traveled back here in the shape of a wolf. Pinocula had just been resting on the island when Trevor found him.

Pinocula apologized for all the lying he had done from the start. He admitted that he wasn't supposed to have busted out of the closet in the first place. According to him, he had left the closet when he shouldn't have. I was supposed to have been visited by a different creature before him. He said the things I learned about him in the books I read were a happy accident. At the end of his speech he told Trevor and me that he now wanted to travel the world and bite famous wooden objects.

WELCOME TO THE
REDWOOD FOREST
ALL-U-CAN-BITE BUFFET

THIS IS GOING
TO BE DELICIOUS!

Jack popped up at my window.

I pointed to Pinocula, and Jack climbed in. I filled Jack in on what was happening while Trevor tried to reason with Pinocula. I liked Pinocula a lot, but of all my visitors so far, he stressed me out the most. He had been here less than a week, but it felt like a year. As we were arguing, something strange began to happen.

My closet door started to shake, and Beardy looked worried. We all stepped back and stared. The smile sticker on the bottom of the door seemed to glow and fade. There was a creaking followed by a soft . . .

- CLICK -

We held our breath as the closet door slowly swung out. After it opened a few inches, two heads appeared.

HELLO, ROB. SO NICE TO SEE YOU. IS HE GIVING YOU TROUBLE?

COME ON, PINO. IT WASN'T YOUR TURN.

Wonk and Hairy were back! I was so thrilled to see them. They stepped out of the closet and walked up to me. Wonk hugged my right leg, and Hairy gave me a low five. Then, instead of telling me how much they had missed me, they grabbed Pinocula and began to drag him toward the closet.

I didn't want them to go. I looked around for something or some idea of how to stop them from leaving so quickly.

Wonk and Hairy looked at me kindly.

Wonk reminded me that both he and Hairy had left me something when they were here.

...THERE WILL COME A TIME WHEN YOU WILL NEED ALL THOSE THINGS.

I looked at the top of my dresser where I kept Wonk's cane and Hairy's scarf. Now Pinocula was leaving me a bat-cricket? I had no idea how those items could ever help me. As I stepped closer to stop them from entering the closet, Beardy growled at me.

Pinocula struggled with my former visitors, but in the end Hairy shoved him into the closet with one strong push.

The door closed, and they were gone. I reached for Beardy and grabbed hold of him. I pulled and the closet door opened easily. Just like before there was nothing but a mess inside. There was no sign of any of the creatures that had come out.

I didn't want to close the closet door because I
was scared that if I did, it wouldn't open again.
Beardy, however, didn't want to stay open. He bit my
hand with his tiny brass mouth. As I let go, he
swung the door shut and it locked once again. I
pulled and pounded on the door, but it was no use.
After a minute of silence, Jack spoke.

I looked at my hand where Beardy had bitten me. There was a small mark, but I noticed that the bite I had gotten from Jim four days ago was now completely gone. I had no idea where the mixed-up bat was, but I felt pretty certain I'd see him again.

I thanked Jack for being such a good friend last night. He and Trevor had saved me and Pinocula. Jack told me I owed him. Then he and Trevor left through the window, and I was alone. I cleaned up my room a little so that my parents might go easier on me. As I was tidying up I saw a dark flapping object swoop down and land on the edge of my open window. It was Jim. I figured he was here to see Pinocula.

YOU'RE TOO LATE. HE'S GONE.

I KNEW HE WOULD BE. I TOLD HIM REPEATEDLY THAT HIS LIES WOULD CATCH UP WITH HIM.

Jim chirped like a cricket for a few seconds and flapped his wings. He told me a few nice things as well as a few things he thought I should know. After he had spoken his mind, he tipped his cap as if to say farewell. I asked him where he was going, and he told me that he'd *be* around.

AND REMEMBER, I'M WATCHING YOU.

I shut my window *so* he couldn't watch too closely. I used to *be* scared of Santa Claus. Now, I had Jim watching me too.

I don't think I've ever felt more motivated to behave.

CHAPTER 14

OPPORTUNITIES

After about a half hour of cleaning my room, I opened my bedroom door and hollered,

HELLO, I'M STARVING!

My mom yelled back something about how there were honest children all over the world who were far hungrier than me.

At around eleven o'clock, my dad finally came to my room. He was trying to look serious and stern, but I knew it was a struggle for him. I told him how sorry I was for about the hundredth time.

I started to think about all the stuff I had been through. I guess I learned a few things. Maybe

Pinocula had used me to help him, but I had used a few people to help me as well. I didn't want to end up like Dracula, dead, or Pinocchio, obnoxious. It probably was a wise idea for me to make a few adjustments. Once again my life was different because of books I'd read. I might have figured out things in a roundabout way, but the stories of Dracula and Pinocchio would be with me forever.

My father said a few more things to me that he
thought a dad was supposed to say. He wrapped up
his speech by saying,

My dad left my room and then my mom came in.
It was like they were professional punishers in a
tag-team match. My mom told me all the things I'd
be grounded from and informed me that I'd be
writing apology notes to a lot of people.

My mom gave me a list of all the things I needed to do. The list seemed really long. It all looked painful, but the most painful thing she wanted me to do was at the very top.

Apologizing to Janae was the thing I least wanted to do. I felt horrible about all the lies I had thrown around like a lying super villain.

I felt the worst about Janae. It was impossible to stop thinking about the kiss and how I'd never be able to look her in the eyes again. I took a shower, got dressed, and walked slowly over to her house to apologize. I stood on Janae's porch for at least five minutes before working up the courage to push the doorbell. Her sister, Lisa, answered.

Lisa turned around and went to get Janae. A few minutes later, Janae came to the door. She looked more hurt than mad. I swallowed and began to speak. Before I could get a single syllable out of my mouth, she slammed the door in my face.

I stood there staring at the closed door for a few moments and then turned to walk back home.

In the spirit of being honest, I must say that this is not how I wanted this book to end. I like when the ending of something turns out perfect, like those movies where everybody laughs and dances and sings.

This time, however, I still had a little work to do. Janae had just shut the door in my face, but as my dad always says,

WHEN ONE DOOR SLAMS, ANOTHER DOOR OPENS.

Sure, I wanted to ring Janae's doorbell again and explain my crazy behavior, but I had a feeling that wouldn't help. Maybe I just wasn't ready to understand girls. One door had definitely slammed. Now I just needed to wait for another door to open.

HELLO? ANYONE HOME?

GOFISH

QUESTIONS FOR THE AUTHOR

OBERT SKYE

What sparked your imagination for *Pinocula*? Why did you choose to cross Pinocchio and Dracula?
I always liked Pinocchio because he was mischievous. But he was also unstable and naïve. So it seemed like the wisdom and experience of a vampire would benefit him. Plus, they're both tricky and clever. I also love the thought of a little wooden, lying vampire being added to the mayhem of middle school.

Which characters in the book do you think you are most like? Whom do you most relate to?
Of course I relate to Rob. I have a hard time not getting in trouble or stepping into things that I shouldn't. But I'd love to be more like the vampire part of Pinocula. Cool, confident, and always having something funny to say.

If you heard a strange rattling sound in your closet and discovered a mythical creature there, what's the first thing you would do?
Duck behind my bed and scream. Actually, I'd probably scream and then duck.

What scenes were your favorite to write?
I loved writing this entire book. The dance at the end was *extra* fun to write. School dances make me nervous, so to add Pinocula and TV cameras to the mix was very satisfying.

Who is your favorite fictional character and why?
Willy Wonka. I like how odd he is and that he owns a chocolate factory. My goal is to have my own chocolate factory someday. I want to be like Willy.

Who or what did you most like to doodle when you were young?
I liked to doodle everything. Weird animals were my favorite subjects. I did a comic strip for my school called *Prep-punker*. It was about a goofy, preppy punk rocker. It was kind of my beginning in telling stories with pictures.

What kind of books did you enjoy most when you were young?
I loved anything funny and exciting. Those were my two favorite types of books to read then and now. I loved when a book made me laugh and caused my heart to beat fast. I always try to make my books have a lot of humor and exciting things happening in them.

Can you tell us a little about what to expect in *Katfish*? (No spoilers, please!)
Regular life is awkward enough for Rob. Add all the creatures who have already popped out of his closet and his life is a funny mess. Now, when the first girl character emerges, things get even funnier. I think that Katfish is his biggest challenge—and possibly the most rewarding.

After his adventures with Pinocula, Rob Burnside needs help because no one wants anything to do with him. Of course, his closet is there and soon out comes Katfish, a cross between Katniss from *The Hunger Games* and *The Little Mermaid*. What could possibly go wrong?

THE CREATURE FROM MY CLOSET

KATFISH

OBERT SKYE

Keep reading for an excerpt.

CHAPTER 1

MESS

I know, I know—I blew it. Seriously, my life has become the kind of sticky mess that other sticky messes probably gross out about.

Most of the people in my life won't even talk to me at the moment or acknowledge that I exist.

Sadly, being so disliked doesn't mean I can stop writing down or doodling what I'm going through. I would love to be buried by a big pile of leaves or blankets and left alone for the rest of my life, but there are things I have to do.

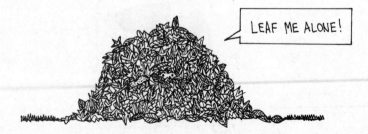

I used to have no interest in books, and I definitely had no desire to write or draw things from my life for scientific purposes. But the world needs to know about my closet and what it can do. So despite being disliked by almost everyone I know at the moment, I must keep writing.

My life is in ruins. I've let my parents down.

My older sister, Libby, hates me just as much as ever.

Janae, the girl I've been crushing on for years, won't even look at me. I could change my style completely and she *still* wouldn't glance my way.

Even my little brother, Tuffin, doesn't look up to me anymore.

Yes, things are uncomfortable. It feels like the time my dad did the laundry and accidentally shrunk all my clothes.

The worst part is that there's nobody to blame but me. I made this mess by lying to all of them about a lot of things. I told them that our school dance was going to be televised and that they were all going to be filmed. I told them they were going to be famous, but in the end, they were just embarrassed. I let everyone down and ruined our first school dance. Principal Smelt gave me detention for fooling everyone.

I don't think there's a single teacher or student at Softrock Middle School who isn't upset with me. Even the school announcements are painful.

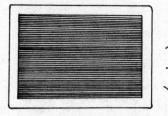

FOR LUNCH TODAY
WE'RE SERVING
PIZZA AND CHICKEN...
AND AS USUAL ROB
BURNSIDE STINKS!

One of the hipster kids at my school even suggested that we change the pledge.

...AND TO THE ROB BURNSIDE, WHO RUINED EVERYTHING, ONE BIG DISAPPOINTMENT...

I wanted to explain to everyone that Pinocula had been the cause of most of the trouble. But the things that came out of my closet weren't really public knowledge, and even if I wanted to spill the beans, Pinocula had returned to the closet and I had no proof of what had gone down.

In an effort to shame me even further, my mom threw an apology party so people could come to our house and I could publicly say I'm sorry. It was a horrible idea. Luckily only one person came—and it wasn't even someone I needed to apologize to. It was just Rex, the homeschooled boy who lived two streets over. He'd heard from someone that there was a party, so he showed up.

He thought it was a birthday party and gave me a gift. I was excited until I opened it.

Rex's mom taught yoga and was big-time into nature stuff. Last summer when Tuffin and I had been playing out in the front yard, she came over and insisted we put on a bunch of homemade sunscreen she had made in her kitchen. I didn't want to, but she stood there until we spread it all on.

It was super sticky and smelled like eggs. We could barely move once it was on. As soon as she left, Tuffin and I ran back and jumped in our swimming pool to wash it off. We splashed and swished, but it didn't come off easily and it made the surface of the pool all oily and yellow. Which was pretty embarrassing when Janae's older sister looked over the fence to see what all the splashing was about.